To Katie, Alice, and Kevin

On the night before Christmas, there was a young mouse
Who was stirring and whirling all through the house.
He longed to see Santa (that jolly old soul),
So he'd stayed awake late and then crept from his hole.

MICHAEL GARLAND

The Mouse Before Christmas

SCHOLASTIC INC.

New York Toronto London Auckland Sydney
Mexico City New Delhi Hong Kong Buenos Aires

ISBN 0-439-70604-1

12 11 10 9 8 7 6 5 4 3 2   6 7 8 9/0

Printed in the U.S.A.   08

First Scholastic printing, November 2004

Designed by Riki Levinson

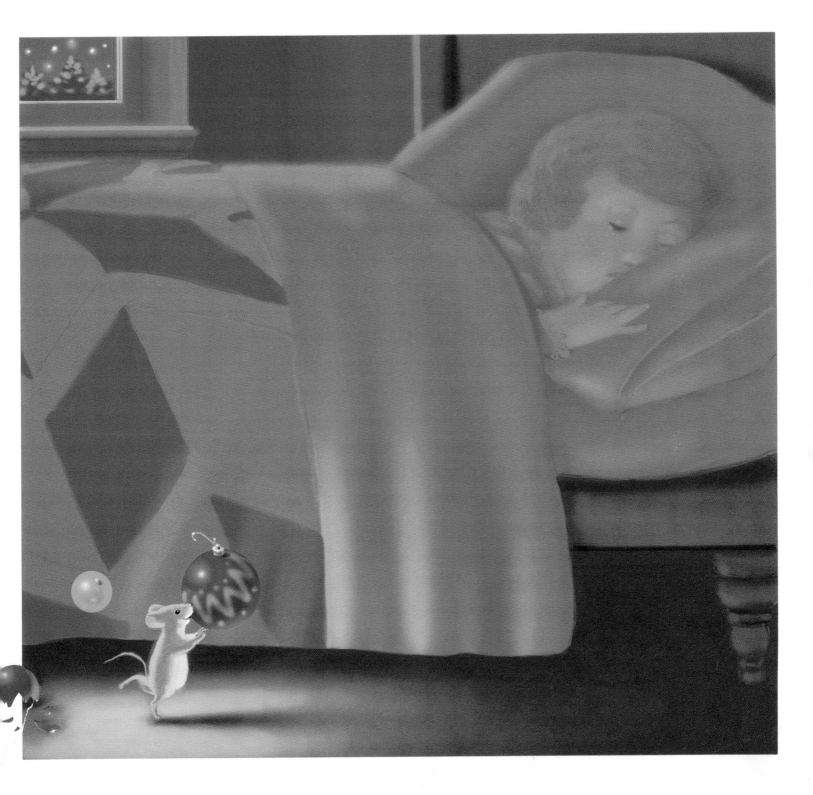

Out in the kitchen, Mouse stacked up a treat:
Chocolate-chip cookies for Santa to eat.

He made not a sound as he hurried and scurried.
But Puss was asleep, so he needn't have worried.

Now on to the fireplace—Mouse gave a sigh;
Though the cookies were heavy, he held the plate high.

Next, where to hide? Mouse looked around quick;
Snug in a pot he could spy on Saint Nick.

Mouse waited and wondered and almost dozed off
Until hoofbeats and sleighbells came from aloft.
From out of the fireplace—*bang, crash,* and *tumble*—
Popped merry old Nick in a heap and a jumble.

Mouse was delighted—his wish had come true.
But what *now*? he wondered. What *more* could he do?
As Nick stuffed the stockings (which started to sag),
Mouse tippy-toed near for a peek in his bag.

Soon Santa was done. Time to hurry away—
He snatched up his sack and sprang out to his sleigh.
With a *swoosh* and a *swish,* Mouse was bundled inside.
But down in the darkness was no place to ride.
"It's stuffy! It's crowded!" Mouse started to shout.
And he squeezed, wiggled, scrambled to find a way out.

He soon spied a place to poke his head free,
Then beheld all around him sights splendid to see.
He was high above Earth in the winter night sky,
Streaking past stars in a sleigh that could fly.
Mouse loved this new feeling, and when he looked down,
Far distant below shone the lights of his town.

Onto rooftops, down chimneys, old Santa did race.
Mouse marveled the reindeer could keep up the pace.
They soared past high mountains, skimmed low near a river.
The twists, dips, and turns set his tummy aquiver.

Over bridges and castles and towers they flew;
The rooftops of London gave Mouse a great view.

Thrilling sights waited in each foreign land.
In Holland the windmills by moonlight looked grand.

Mouse had never imagined a world so wide;
He lost count of the wonders he'd seen on this ride—

Crossing cities and countries, over desert and sea,
Past the sphinx and two towers and Miss Liberty.

At the end of the night, at the very last house,
Santa peeked in his sack. "Why, what's that? A young mouse!"
Mouse was so startled, he feared he'd just squeak;
But in Santa's kind gaze, he found he could speak.
"Oh, Santa, I'm sorry for sneaking this ride,
But your bag was so tempting, I climbed right inside."

Santa just chuckled. "Little friend, don't you worry!
Hop on my hat. You'll be home in a hurry."
Mouse clung to the fringe—the wind chilled his face.
The rocketlike sleigh zoomed and hurtled through space.

Back home, safe and sound, there were presents for all.
The one Mouse liked best was a hat marked size SMALL.
Then Santa crouched down till his beard touched the floor.
The friends waved good-bye through the little front door.

It was *so* late at night, Mouse was ready for bed,
But he wanted to try his new hat on his head.
It was just the right size: not too big, not too small.
A hat just like Santa's! Mouse felt proud and tall.

Mouse snuggled down, letting dreams fill his eyes.
Hearing words meant for him from a voice deep and wise.
"If you do all the things that a good mouse should do,
Don't be surprised when your wishes come true.
Merry Christmas, dear Mouse, Merry Christmas to you."